OTHER PEOP

Wendy Douthwaite lives with her husband near Bristol where they run an art gallery. She has written a number of pony stories including *All Because of Polly* (the sequel to *Other People's Ponies*).

OTHER PEOPLE'S PONIES

Wendy Douthwaite

Illustrated by Joan Thompson

PIPER
PAN MACMILLAN
CHILDREN'S BOOKS

First published 1989 by Macmillan Children's Books

This Piper edition published 1993 by Pan Macmillan Children's Books
a division of Pan Macmillan Publishers Limited
Cavaye Place London SW10 9PG
and Basingstoke

Associated companies throughout the world

ISBN 0 330 32540 X

1 3 5 7 9 8 6 4 2

A CIP catalogue record for this book is available from
the British Library

Typeset by Matrix, Covent Garden, London WC2
Printed by Cox & Wyman Ltd, Reading, Berkshire

One

"I'm sorry, Jess, it's out of the question."

"But, Dad—"

Across the supper table, Mr Caswell looked at his eldest daughter with eyes that were reproachful and even a little irritated, but when he spoke again his voice was quiet and understanding.

"Jess, you *know* I'm not saying this without having given the matter plenty of thought, but I have to tell you that we cannot afford to buy you a pony." He looked around the table, almost defiantly, at the four other members of the family.

They were unusually quiet. Everyone knew, including Dad, how desperately Jess wanted a pony, how the love of ponies and the longing for a pony of her own had become almost an obsession. Even Thomas, the youngest of the Caswell children, who was not quite four, had grown up with the idea that one day Jess would have a pony. He was constantly finding photographs of ponies in newspapers and magazines, which he would cut out carefully and bring to her, beaming with pleasure.

1

"There you are, Dess," he would say, not having yet managed the art of pronouncing the letter J, "p'raps that's your pony!"

When Dad had been promised promotion at work, the family had moved from the semi-detached house in Catley where they fitted tightly into three bedrooms and one living room. Jess had been filled with hope. The cottage at Edgecombe, twelve miles out into the country, seemed like paradise to all six members of the Caswell family. Four bedrooms and a boxroom meant that each of the three girls had a room of her own and Thomas, together with his clockwork train and soft toys, was accommodated snugly by the boxroom.

Jess had been sure that her dream was about to come true when Dad had taken them all to see Trumpeter Cottage, just two months ago, on a chilly February afternoon. They had stood in the frost-festooned front garden of the cottage, their breath forming small white clouds in the cold air. Thomas had chugged up and down the path, panting noisily and pretending to be a steam engine. In a voice that could not hide his excitement, Dad had told them that if Mum liked the cottage, too, then they could just about afford it.

The four Caswell children had followed their parents in a little straggly group, as they inspected the empty cottage. Eleven-year-old Jess, holding Tom's hand tightly, had been quiet, whilst inside her head she had repeated the words, Please let them buy it, oh, *please* let them buy it! For Jess had seen the small, rough-looking stable next to a stone shed, and the gate leading into an orchard. And Dad had looked at her, smiling, and nodding his head in the direction of the stable. *Surely*, it was all going to work out, and she would have her pony at last?

Clare and Kim, walking just behind her, talked in quick, excited whispery voices, and Jess knew that they had fallen under the spell of Trumpeter Cottage as she had. But would Mum love it? However, it did not take long to know how Mum felt. By the time they had reached the kitchen with its old range and long windows looking out over the back garden and beyond to one end of the orchard, Mum's eyes were shining. She sat in the deep window seat and looked across the room at Dad.

"We can do *so much* with this room," Mum said.

"The cottage will need a lot doing to it," Dad reminded her, trying to sound cautious, but not succeeding as he continued quickly, "but I can do most of it myself. The biggest job will be the plumbing, but that won't be too difficult – just time-consuming and perhaps a bit messy. The roof is sound and there's no damp. Most of the work will be decorating and fitting cupboards – things like that."

"I can do lots of that in the daytime, when you're at work," Mum put in, excitedly, "and the children will help, won't you?"

An excited babble followed, during which it was generally agreed that Trumpeter Cottage should and would belong to the Caswell family.

Now, as Jess sat in that same kitchen, staring down hard at her half-cleared plate and making an effort not to cry, she could not understand what was going wrong. Through the misery which hammered in her head, she heard Dad's voice explaining, and gradually the words seeped through. ". . . the promotion just hasn't come . . . the firm's going through a sticky patch . . . some of the others are even being made redundant—"

"Dad!" Jess looked up quickly, forgetting her own misery. "They're not going to make *you* redundant, are they?"

"No, it's all right, Jessie," Dad replied. ".My job's safe enough as long as the firm stays in business." He looked round at them all again. "But I'm afraid it means no promotion for me just now, and that means that we'll have to be very careful not to over-spend." He looked at his wife. "I think they're all old enough to understand, don't you, Jan?" Mrs Caswell nodded, and he continued, "We all like it here, don't we?" He did not need to wait for a reply, but talked on, "Well, it was a much more expensive house to buy than our old one, and we do need to spend some money on it – and that means we can't buy luxuries. And ponies *are* luxuries. I'm sorry, Jess. Perhaps if things get better at work . . ."

Jess didn't cry that night as she lay in bed. It all seemed too important for crying. Moonlight streamed in through the half-open curtains, dimly lighting the square, cottagey bedroom which Jess was still not quite used to having as her own room. She looked at it with pleasure, her eyes wandering past the peeling paint on the thick, uneven walls, to the plentiful array of horse and pony posters which she had pinned up on her first day at the cottage.

On one wall of the room a deep recess held shelves, which Jess had filled with books and her ornaments – mostly of ponies. She gazed at the small figures sleepily. Sometimes she imagined her china ponies coming to life during the night and cantering about her room, leaping lightly on to the window sill, where they would snort and paw the wooden sill impatiently. The grey arab, which was her favourite, would poke his dainty nose in the air and whinny shrilly.

Jess felt her eyes closing as sleep gradually claimed her. She would think about her problem tomorrow. For now, the arab had grown to full size, and he was standing impatiently at the orchard gate, tossing his beautiful head and waiting for her to ride him . . .

Two

"It's awful!"

"What is?" Jess looked sideways at nine-year-old Clare, who sat next to her on the wall, swinging her legs to kick angrily at the stonework.

"Dad's saving money thing, of course," her sister replied, hunching her shoulders miserably. "He's going to let me keep on with my ballet lessons at school, but Mum said this morning that I can't keep up the extra Saturday morning ones."

Eight-year-old Kim looked up from the grassy bank below the wall, where she was sitting cross-legged, carefully making a daisy-chain. "Well, *I* was going to start having violin lessons next term and I can't now," she stated.

"Dad can't *help* it," Jess reminded them.

" 'Course he can't," agreed Kim, stoically, "and Tom has had to stop going to play-school, so we're all in the same boat, aren't we?"

"But how am I going to become a famous ballet dancer, if I can't have lessons?" wailed Clare from her lofty position.

"Oh, Clare, don't be such a *pain*," Jess said, impatiently. "It doesn't help to moan. At least you're having *some* lessons."

7

Although offended by Jess's comment, Clare was silent. She remembered, suddenly, that Jess had been having a riding lesson once a week when they had lived at Catley, but since the move to Edgecombe she had not ridden at all.

Jess gazed meditatively across the lane to the field opposite, where a herd of young heifers grazed. "You know, I'm sure I could ride one of those, if I put my halter on it," she mused. Clare and Kim had given Jess a rope halter for Christmas. "I read about someone who rides her cows when they get too old for milking," Jess continued. "She had saddles for them, too!"

Kim looked up at her elder sister. "You wouldn't *really*, would you, Jess?" she asked, in awed tones.

"If I get desperate enough," Jess replied, grinning at her as she slid down from the wall. "Come on, here's the school bus!"

Kim had already made several friends in her class at their new school, and she disappeared into the crowded depths of the school bus when it pulled up alongside the three girls. Clare and Jess sat at the back. Clare had made one friend, who came to school on a different bus, but Jess, with her quiet and diffident ways, had found it difficult to make new friends. She discovered that everyone in the fourth form seemed to have at least one close friend and, although they were friendly enough, most of the time Jess found herself sitting alone or wandering by herself in the playground at break times.

Today, she did not really mind too much, for she felt that she wanted to think hard about her knotty problem. How was she ever going to have a pony of her own – and indeed, how could she even find some way of riding? There seemed to be no riding stables close by at Edgecombe, and she couldn't ask Dad to drive her to Catley every week, just so that she could have an hour's ride – and anyway riding lessons were so expensive and . . . Jess, who had been wandering, head lowered, across the playground, came suddenly and painfully into contact with the tall wire fence at the edge of the playground.

"Ouch!"

"My goodness, you *were* deep in thought!" said an amused voice close by. Looking up, Jess saw that the speaker was Miss Claremont, her form teacher. Jess grinned sheepishly. She liked Miss Claremont, who was young and full of enthusiasm.

"Seems like quite a problem you're trying to work out," Miss Claremont continued, stepping a little nearer. Then she added, "Do you want any help – or is it private?"

"Well . . ." Jess hesitated. It would probably seem a silly sort of problem to a teacher. They tended to disapprove of passionate feelings about ponies, she had found, for teachers felt that if you thought about ponies you wouldn't be thinking about your school work. Still, Miss Claremont seemed nice. She hesitated again, and then told her. As Miss Claremont listened, her eyes were surprisingly sympathetic, Jess thought, and when Jess had finished her story, Miss Claremont laughed delightedly.

"Well, you know," she said, "you just couldn't have told a better person than me because, you see, *I* love ponies too. I had one when I was young." Miss Claremont's eyes became dreamy. "He was a lovely little chestnut, with a white blaze and one white sock, and his name was—" She stopped suddenly. "Goodness, I mustn't ramble on like this."

"No, really, I don't mind," said Jess quickly. "He sounds lovely—"

"Yes, I know, but we were discussing your problem," interrupted Miss Claremont, "and I think I might be able to help you."

A loud clanging interrupted her. "Oh dear, there's the bell," she said. "We'll have to go in." Miss Claremont turned towards the staff room, saying hurriedly, "I'll see you here after lunch, Jess, and I might have some good news for you . . ."

The rest of the morning and lunchtime seemed interminable. Jess felt puzzled by Miss Claremont's words, and yet the teacher's voice had

10

sounded so optimistic. Jess just could not imagine what Miss Claremont had in mind. At last it was the lunchtime break, and Jess hurried out to meet the promiser of good tidings.

Miss Claremont was waiting in the same corner of the playground where they had met that morning, and Jess was surprised to see a girl from one of the other fourth-year classes with her.

Miss Claremont smiled warmly at Jess. "Oh good," she said, "you're here already. I've got to rush. Now, Jess, this is Rachel Fielding. She can tell you all about it. I'm due in the staff room for a meeting. 'Bye, both of you!" And in a moment she had vanished through the milling throngs of schoolchildren.

Rachel grinned at Jess. "Always on the go is Miss Claremont," she commented.

"She's nice, though, isn't she?" said Jess, feeling awkward and shy.

"Oh, yes, she's great," agreed Rachel. There was a small silence, then Rachel continued, "Well, I gather you've got a field and no pony?" Jess nodded. "Well," continued Rachel, cheerfully, "I've got a pony with no one to look after him for two months – so perhaps we should get together!"

"It's a temporary loan, you see, Dad. Rachel's father's a lecturer, and the whole family is going

11

to America for two months on an exchange. Rachel will have the pony shod before she goes, and he shouldn't really *cost* me anything. He won't need feeding, now it's April. And Rachel says if by any chance he's ill, I can put the vet's charges on their account. And he's *never* ill, anyway, she said. So, I *can*, can't I, Dad? *Please* say yes!"

Jess was breathless after her eloquent speech. Everyone turned towards Dad, who looked taken aback.

"You're all looking at me as if I were some sort of ogre!" he laughed. "Of *course* you can have him, Jess – you didn't really think I would say no, did you?"

All at once the kitchen was filled with noise, as everyone talked at once. Even Badger, the family dog, who was middle-aged and portly, raised himself up from beside the kitchen range and came over to see what was happening. He pushed his nose under Mum's hand and waved his tail, as if to say "Am I missing something?"

"What colour is he?" asked Mum, absently stroking Badger's black and white head.

Jess, pink with suppressed excitement, shrugged her shoulders. "I don't know," she admitted. "I didn't ask Rachel."

"How big is he?" asked practical Kim.

"About fourteen hands."

"What's he called?" Clare asked.

"Beetle." Everyone shrieked with laughter.

"Is he nice?" piped up Tom.

Jess looked a little doubtful. "I don't know," she said. "I hope so. Rachel just said that he was a bit of a handful. But I don't care," she added happily, "if he's only got three legs! I'm going to have a pony at last!"

Three

It wasn't exactly love at first sight. As Rachel
led Beetle down the ramp from the horse-box, his
ears were flattened firmly against his head and his
eyes rolled menacingly. He hesitated at the top of
the ramp, then careered down, dragging Rachel
with him.

"He's quite strong," Rachel panted, when
they reached firm ground. "There's a good
old boy," she soothed, patting his neck, which
rippled with muscles. "He *hates* horse-boxes,"
she explained to Jess. "Ouch! Stop it, Bee!"
Beetle had stretched his neck to nip Rachel
on the arm. She rubbed her arm, explaining
with a wry smile, "He's always giving me these
affectionate little nibbles – he doesn't realise they
hurt!"

Rachel inclined her head towards the front of
the horse-box. "All the gear's in the front," she
told Jess. "If you get it out, you can have a ride
– see what you think of him."

All at once, Jess became conscious of her
family gathered around Beetle, and of Mr Fielding, who had driven the horse-box and who was
now watching with interest.

"Er . . . perhaps it might be kinder to put him in his field," Jess suggested. "Let him get used to his new surroundings."

"OK," agreed Rachel cheerfully. "Perhaps you're right. He does get a bit uppity after a trip in the box. Come on then, Bee, old thing."

As Jess hurried off to collect the saddlery, she was aware of Rachel tugging at Beetle's head-collar, and of Beetle's stubborn, resisting stance. However, by the time she had returned, weighed down by the saddle, two bridles, a martingale, extra reins and bits, a halter and a bucket, she found that Rachel had persuaded Beetle to walk towards the orchard. Hurrying on ahead to store the saddlery in the shed, Jess then opened the orchard gate, and Beetle walked suspiciously into his new home.

The two girls, flanked by the various family members, watched Beetle from the gate as he wandered about the orchard, snatching a mouthful of grass here and there and sniffing and snorting, apprehensively.

"I hope you two get on together," Rachel said, quietly. "He's a stubborn old thing, is Beetle, but I love him."

Jess watched the sleek, dark bay pony as he wandered about the orchard. "Well," she replied with candour, "we can only try. But I'll look after him, I promise," she added, "and it *is* lovely to have him – a pony to ride at last!"

15

When everyone had gone, Jess made her way to the orchard again. It was late evening, and the sun was setting behind the old apple trees, casting long, crooked shadows across the grass. Beetle was quieter now, cropping the grass steadily in the open, treeless part of the orchard. Sitting on the top bar of the gate, Jess listened contentedly to the rhythmical munching, and watched Beetle's long black tail swishing. She daydreamed, imagining that Beetle was the grey arab. In her mind she saw him raise his head sharply, then throw it up and whinny loud and strong, before trotting over towards her with his high, flowing gait, halting beside her and pushing his soft nose into her hand. Beetle just raised his head slightly, peering at her without much interest before putting his head down again to get on with the important business of eating.

Never mind, Jess thought, back in the real world again, it's a start.

Jess leaned against one of the apple trees, exhausted, then slid her back down to sit dejectedly on the sun-warmed grass at its base. "I mustn't get annoyed," she told herself firmly, "that will mean that he's getting the better of me." She tightened her grip on the lead-rope as her inner feelings belied what she was telling herself. She *was* annoyed! He was just playing a game with her. Each time she approached him, holding out the carrot she had brought, whilst hiding the lead-rope behind her back, Beetle would walk nonchalantly away from her, watching her out of the corner of one eye. If she increased her pace, he increased his, and if she slowed down, so did Beetle. They had continued this exasperating game for nearly an hour. Jess had expected to be out on the lanes by now, but here she was still in the orchard with nothing but the lead-rope and an inquisitive robin to keep her company – and the back-end of Beetle, of course!

At a safe distance, Beetle cropped the grass placidly, keeping a wary eye on Jess in case she should begin again. He enjoyed this game, she could tell. He had played it many times before, obviously, and was a master at the art of evading being ridden. But she wouldn't be beaten! Resolutely, Jess stood up, ready to begin again. Beetle stopped munching and prepared to resume. Then both their attentions were diverted by a small figure, hurrying across the grass towards them, calling out,

"Dess! Dess! You forgot this!"

It was Tom, beaming his special little three-year-old beam, and staggering under the weight and bulk of Beetle's bucket.

"I put some grass in it," Tom confided, panting as he arrived at her side, " 'cos ponies *like* grass."

Jess rumpled his straight golden hair affectionately. He was so sweet sometimes! "Thanks,

18

Tommy," she said, gently, "but I don't think the bucket will—" As she spoke, a dark brown nose pushed down between them, towards the bucket. Quickly overcoming her surprise, Jess reached out and snapped the end of the lead-rope round the metal ring in the head-collar. At last she had him!

Jess hummed to herself as she brushed Beetle's already shining hindquarters. I must buy some pony nuts, she thought, as she brushed down towards his hocks. He's not going to think much of grass in his bucket every time – and the bucket's obviously the way to bribe him into being caught. Oh dear, she sighed, expense already! Seeing Beetle's hind leg raised ominously when she reached towards his tail to brush it, she decided that it looked all right as it was!

Leaving Beetle tied up outside the stable, munching at the hay-filled bag that Rachel had left – goodness! I'll have to buy a bale of hay, too! she thought – Jess fetched the saddle and bridle from the shed. Tom was her only watcher, sitting on the warm flagstones outside the shed, running his little metal cars through the earth between the stones, whilst emitting the appropriate car-engine noises.

"Are you going for a ride?" he asked.

"I hope so," Jess replied, hanging the bridle on a hook outside the stable. "But I can't be sure of anything with *this* pony," she added, winking at Tom over the saddle. She lifted the saddle and rested it on Beetle's withers before sliding it down to its correct position on his back. Then, she reached under his belly for the end of the girth, which hung down on the other side. Beetle stopped munching and kicked upwards with one hind leg. Annoyed, Jess smacked him. "Stop it!" she commanded crossly. "You're very bad-mannered!" Beetle seemed surprised, and stood looking quite disconsolate, so Jess patted his neck, speaking more gently to him as he resumed his munching.

Having fastened the girth and pulled down the stirrup irons, Jess fetched the bridle from its hook and eyed the opposition carefully. There was no doubt about it – she was going to have to remove the head-collar before she could put on the bridle. Slipping the reins over Beetle's neck and holding them under his chin, Jess unbuckled the head-collar warily, waiting for Beetle to attempt to escape. But, much to her surprise, Beetle waited quite patiently while the bit was eased into his mouth and the headpiece pulled over his ears and settled into position. Jess buckled the throatlash, and they were ready to go.

"He doesn't seem to want to stand still," Tom pointed out, helpfully, from his playground on the flagstones, after Jess's fourth attempt at mounting Beetle.

"I can see that," muttered Jess through clenched teeth. Then in a sharp voice, she said, "Beetle! Stand *still* will you!"

He didn't exactly stand still, but there was a small moment without too much movement, during which Jess was able to jump into the saddle. As they trotted off down the drive, Jess found the stirrups and collected the reins.

" 'Bye, Tommy," she called. Then to Beetle, she said, "You really were badly brought up, you know."

Beetle merely snorted and cocked one ear back in Jess's direction, before testing her out with a large buck.

"Hah! I was ready for you!" Jess panted, triumphantly, as she again scrambled to regain the stirrups. She eased gently on the reins, slowing Beetle to a walk. "Now then," she continued, "we're going to walk for a while and then *I'm* going to decide when we trot!"

Four

Mum was out in the garden when Jess arrived back from the two-hour ride.

"How was he?" she asked, straightening up from weeding a flower border.

"Well, I'll say one thing for him," Jess commented, as she slid down from the saddle, "he's got character! Trouble is," she added, ruefully, "I can't quite decide what it is – bad or good!"

Mum strolled over to pat Beetle's sleek, dark neck. "He seems docile enough now," she said. "Ouch!" She backed away, rubbing her arm.

"Sorry, Mum, but that's one of his characteristics!"

However, Jess's spirits were high as she led Beetle towards the stable. It had been wonderful to be riding again, and a two-hour ride was luxurious! She had discovered on that first ride that Beetle was a difficult pony – moody and unpredictable. One minute he would be plodding sluggishly along the lane and the next he would be dancing sideways, acting like a two year old, having seen an imaginary piece of paper in the hedge. For some of the ride he had felt alert, his ears had been pricked and he had looked about him with interest. Then, suddenly, he would begin to plod, his ears would droop and when Jess leaned forward to talk to him, his expression was sour.

"What you need is a horse psychiatrist!" Jess told him, cheerily, as she removed the saddle. Beetle stretched out his neck and nipped her thigh.

"Ouch! You *horrible* pony!"

Jess leaned against his warm shoulder and considered Beetle thoughtfully. "You're not exactly *vicious*, Beetle," she told him, "you're just . . . crafty and underhand," she finished, laughing, as she unbuckled the bridle and took it off, replacing it with the head-collar. She patted him. "You're not *so* bad, really, are you, old boy. I begin to see what Rachel meant. And I do know *one* thing you like, don't I?" she added.

Jess had discovered, quite by accident, that Beetle had one passion. They had been trotting along a grass verge and had come to a drainage channel cut in the grass. Jess had expected Beetle to just trot over it, but he pricked his ears when he saw it, and took a tremendous leap over it, nearly unseating her. When she had turned him round to take him over it again, this time at a canter, his pleasure at jumping was evident. He had been in one of his plodding moods but, after the jump, he jogged along the lane, alert and lively and a pleasure to ride. Later on, up on the common, Jess had found a small jump that some other riders had built – just a small, rough brush fence. This jump was a source of delight to Beetle, who jumped it time and time again, giving a little buck of delight just before each take-off.

Now, as Jess closed the orchard gate, leaving Beetle cropping the grass, her mind was full of plans. Certainly Beetle was not a perfect pony, but Jess, who was wise beyond her years at times, did not expect perfection.

She looked at Beetle's shining hindquarters, watching his tail swishing rhythmically as he moved slowly away from her through the grass, and her heart was full of happiness. A field and a pony in it which she could ride – that was all Jess asked of life at present. Of course, her *own* pony would be wonderful but . . . Jess kept her mind on the attainable. Tomorrow, she would begin to build a jump in the orchard.

The letter from Rachel arrived on Monday morning, in the last week of term. The three Caswell sisters were late for the school bus.

"Come *on*, Jess. We'll miss it!" Clare called over her shoulder as she ran down the path, her school satchel bouncing on her back.

Kim paused in the doorway. "What are you doing, Jess? You know he won't wait!"

"I'm just seeing if there's anything for me," Jess replied, leafing through the letters which had dropped through the front door letter-box and lay scattered on the mat. "Ah! Here we are. Come on – race you!"

Still breathless, Jess read the letter in the school bus. Rachel's letter, written in large and untidy handwriting, was full of enthusiasm for America and the Americans.

"What does she say?" asked Clare from her seat next to Jess.

"She loves it," Jess replied, distractedly, as she struggled to decipher Rachel's erratic scrawl. After a pause, she added, "She's been to two barbecues."

Clare saw a new friend of hers at the front of the bus, and moved to a seat further up to talk to her, so Jess was able to settle down to her letter without interruption.

"How's dear old Bee?" Rachel's cheerful letter read. "I *do* miss him – difficult and awkward though he is. I forgot to tell you something about him – he *loves* jumping!" Jess smiled to herself, and then resumed her reading. "He can be quite good at it, too," Rachel's letter continued, "if he's in the mood! I usually enter him at Upper Edgecombe Horse Show at the Spring Bank Holiday in May, and since I won't be back, perhaps you'd like to have a go? I expect there'll be a poster about the show

25

in the window at Edgecombe Post Office – there usually is."

Jess finished Rachel's letter, which continued to expound with enthusiasm upon the American way of life. Then she leaned back in her seat and daydreamed. She saw herself and Beetle flying over huge fences, watched by an admiring and cheering crowd. In a haze of contentment, Jess thought of nearly three weeks of holidays ahead, with Beetle to ride every day. Gradually, she became aware of a voice in her ear, and someone dug her in the ribs.

"I'm not *that* keen to get to school!" said the voice, accompanied by giggles from someone else, "but we're here!"

Awakened from her daydreams, Jess grinned sheepishly, and hurried to make her way down the bus.

Five

It was Mum who found the notice about Muffin.

On the first day of the Easter holidays – which turned out to be rather eventful – Jess was awake early. The sky was grey when she looked out of her bedroom window, but with a faint mistiness which promised sunshine later. Quickly pulling on jodhpurs and a shirt, Jess made her way down to the kitchen. Badger thumped his tail lazily from his bed by the old range. He raised his head to look at Jess with sleepily surprised eyes, before heaving a sigh and going back to sleep. Badger was a creature of habit, and six-thirty on an April morning was half an hour too early for him to think about waking up!

Jess filled the electric kettle and switched it on. She splashed her face with cold water at the sink. The bathroom upstairs was in the sort of chaos that can only get better, since Dad was busy at weekends and in the evenings, replumbing and decorating. For the present, the Caswell family had to manage with the only usable tap in the kitchen sink, or the old baby bath, filled with water from the kettle and taken upstairs for a "lick and promise" wash!

As Jess laid the tray with cups and saucers for tea to take upstairs, she looked out of the kitchen window. Behind the orchard, the sky glowed faintly pink as the sun rose, dispersing the mist. It was going to be a lovely day! Feeling that she must not waste a minute of these holidays – her first with her own pony to ride – Jess hastily made the tea. Well, maybe he wasn't quite her own pony, she reminded herself. However, she thought, philosophically, as she added the teapot, milk and biscuit tin to the tray, the best thing was to live for the present, and, for the present, Beetle, with all his faults, belonged to her!

Having surprised her parents with the tray of tea, Jess persuaded Badger to relinquish the comfort of his bed.

"You're getting much too fat and lazy," Jess told him sternly. Badger looked at her with the patient calm of middle age, and wagged his tail in agreement.

"I'll take you for a walk before breakfast," she told him. At the sound of the magic word, Badger bounced his fat form around the kitchen, as excited as a puppy.

"Poor old Badge," said Jess, fondly, "I've been neglecting you, haven't I, with all the excitement of moving and having a pony." She clipped on his lead. "Come on then – Keep Fit time!"

Outside the air was cool and crisp. The sound of birdsong was everywhere. Jess and

Badger visited Beetle in the orchard, and then began their walk down the quiet country lane.

"I'll let you off the lead when we get to the track," Jess promised – and then her heart stood still. Beside the road lay a small tabby cat, curled up just as though it were asleep. But Jess could see that it was not asleep; it was dead, probably hit by a car driven carelessly, maybe, and too fast through the night.

"Poor little thing," Jess sighed, looking down at the little tabby cat. It looked very thin and shabby. Maybe it had been a stray, Jess thought. It looked peaceful, curled up in the grass, so she left it there. A few yards further on, a grassy track meandered down to join the lane, and here Jess released Badger from his lead.

Bounding off, Badger was soon lost from sight, but Jess could hear his ample form crashing through the undergrowth. She grinned to herself – that would do him good! Jess wandered on, enjoying the walk along the grassy path. Then she became aware of Badger barking. It was not just an occasional bark – it was the determined, excited bark of a dog who has found something really interesting. Badger was part-retriever. What had he found now? Turning off the path, Jess followed the sound of the barking until she came to a small clearing. There was Badger, standing next to an old tree stump, barking and wagging his tail, furiously.

"Badger, whatever have you – Oh!"

Looking down into the hollow part of the tree stump, Jess saw three tiny, wriggling creatures in a nest of bracken and dried grass. At first, she could not decide what they were, and then she realised – they were very young kittens. Immediately, Jess understood what must have happened. The little stray tabby cat had been looking after her three kittens in this quiet wood, and had been killed whilst out foraging for food. These three blind, wriggling lumps were orphans, and needed food and warmth urgently.

"Badger, you clever old boy," Jess said, patting him, "if you hadn't found them, they would have died." Picking up the kittens carefully, one by one, Jess transferred them to the bottom of her shirt, which she held in a cradle shape with her left hand. Two of the kittens meowed plaintively, but the third – the smallest – was quiet and hardly moved.

"We shall have to get you home quickly," Jess murmured. Obviously, this was the weakest of the litter and was already beginning to lose its strength.

Carrying the orphans carefully, Jess made her way back through the copse to the path, and then to the lane, accompanied by an attentive

Badger. He was very interested in these new acquisitions, and seemed to feel that they were his responsibility.

"You'd better stay with me," Jess told him. "I can't manage you on your lead *and* these three." But Badger was far too intrigued by the kittens to wander, and they all arrived home safely.

Dad was setting off for work when Jess and Badger reached the front door. He peered in at the contents of Jess's makeshift cradle and grinned at his eldest daughter. "We shall have to buy a bigger place, Jess, if you bring much more home," he chuckled. "I hope you manage to save them," he added, as he turned towards the garage, "that little ginger one looks as if it's on the way out."

Jess's heart twisted painfully. The smallest kitten mustn't die!

"Mum!" she called, "I've got something to show you!"

Mum assessed the situation quickly. Soon, the three kittens were in a cardboard box on top of the range, with some old sheeting packed around them, and Kim had been sent in search of dolls' feeding bottles. Although slightly ashamed of the fact, since she felt that she should have outgrown them by now, Kim still rather liked her dolls, and three usable feeding bottles were soon found.

"Here we are then, girls," said Mum, as she carefully poured warmed, diluted milk into the tiny bottles, "one each."

"I'll feed the little ginger one," said Jess quickly.

"Mm . . ." said Mum, "I'm not sure he's going to live, though, Jess."

Clare and Kim were soon able to feed the two tabbies, but the ginger kitten seemed uninterested in the doll's bottle that was presented to him.

"*Please* drink some," said Jess, anxiously, as the milk dribbled down past the kitten's mouth.

"I'll try opening his mouth," said Mum, "and you see if you can get some down him then. We'll have to force him, I'm afraid."

By this method they managed to persuade some milk to dribble down the ginger kitten's throat, but Mum looked doubtful. "They'll need feeding every couple of hours, I expect," she said, "but this one will need looking at every half an hour at first, I think, if we're going to save him."

"I'll look after him," Jess promised. "I'll set the timer!"

"All right," said Mum. "Come and have your breakfast. The kittens will be warm and comfortable on the range. I've got something to show *you*, now!"

Whilst Jess helped herself to cereal and milk and sat down next to Clare at the kitchen table, Mum fetched the local paper, which

had been delivered that morning. She turned to the middle pages and then handed the paper to Jess.

"There – what about that, Jess?" she asked, pointing to one of the small advertisements. Under the heading "Livestock", one of the items read, "Temporary home wanted for much-loved family pony while owner at college."

Jess looked up at her mother. "Do you think I could?" she said, excitedly.

"What is it?" asked Kim, through a mouthful of cornflakes.

"Someone wants a temporary home for a pony," Jess explained, her mind racing ahead. Beetle would be going home in six weeks' time – and how lovely, anyway, to have two ponies! But what about the cost of another pony? Jess frowned. "But maybe we can't afford it," she added, thoughtfully.

"Well, it wouldn't harm to telephone," Mum pointed out. "If the owner wants you to pay all the expenses, then perhaps we should think again."

"But you've *got* a pony, Dess," said Tommy, looking across the table at his sister with puzzled eyes.

"He'll have to go back to his owner in June," Jess explained. Then she turned to look at her sisters. "I could teach you two to ride!" she exclaimed.

Clare looked aghast. "You're not getting *me* on a pony," she declared emphatically. "I might get bow-legged, and then I couldn't be a famous ballet dancer!"

Kim giggled into her cornflakes. Jess, catching her eye, began to giggle, too, and Clare fled to her bedroom in tears.

"Now, girls, that wasn't very kind," Mum said mildly.

"But, Mum—" Kim began.

"I know," Mum broke in, "Clare takes everything in life too seriously. But that's just the way she is." Mum sighed. "Perhaps it won't harm her to be laughed at a little. She must learn not to take herself too seriously." She looked across the table at the two sisters. "But she *is* good at her ballet, you know," Mum told them. "Mrs Perkins, her ballet teacher, says that Clare is the best pupil she's ever had, and she thinks Clare could go on to do very well, maybe even make it her career."

Kim and Jess looked at each other and Jess pushed back her chair. "Perhaps we ought to go up to her," she said.

In her bedroom upstairs, Clare lay prostrate on the bed. She looked up with a tear-stained face when the other two came in.

"What do you want?" she sniffed.

Jess sat down on the bed. "We weren't laughing at *you*," she explained, diplomatically.

Kim joined in. "It was just the thought of you getting on a pony," she said, trying hard to stifle another giggle, "and then getting off with bent legs!" The giggle broke through, despite Kim's attempt to restrain it, and soon all three girls were laughing helplessly.

A shrill ringing stopped them.

"The timer!" Jess exclaimed. "It's time to feed the kitten again!"

Six

The rest of Jess's day was taken up with feeding the ginger kitten. Every half-hour, the kitchen timer rang shrilly and Jess managed to persuade a little more of the warm milk down the kitten's reluctant throat.

For the first time since he had arrived at Trumpeter Cottage, Beetle was not ridden. When Jess went to see him during the afternoon, he was standing disconsolately at the orchard gate. She only had time to give him a quick pat and to receive a nip on her shoulder, before she returned to the kitten.

At last, at teatime, the ginger kitten began to suck greedily at the doll's bottle, and Mum pronounced him able to be fed at two-hourly intervals.

When Dad came home from work, Jess showed him the newspaper advertisement.

"What do you think, Dad?"

"Jess, you know the problem just now."

"So you don't think I should?"

"Well, if it involves expense," Dad replied, "then I don't think we can consider it. But if the owners just want a home for their pony, and they will pay the expenses, then that's fine." He leaned back in his chair and loosened his tie. "If you do go out to see it, I'm afraid I can't come. I *must* get on with that bathroom."

"I'll borrow Dad's car and take you," said Mum. "But go and telephone first, Jess. The pony might have a home by now."

Jess sat on the gate, watching her two temporary ponies as they grazed together in the orchard, and she could hardly believe her good fortune. Of course, it had all been due to Tommy, really. When the time had come to discuss the expense of keeping Muffin for the next year, Mrs Carter had gazed fondly at Tommy. He had smiled his angelic smile at her and she had been won over.

"Well, you know, Henry," she said, turning to her husband, "we did say the important thing would be that Muffin has a happy home." She turned to smile adoringly at Tommy. "And I'm sure these dear children will look after our little Muffin."

"You see," she confided, turning to Mrs Caswell, "Henry and I are getting on, now – Elizabeth came to us when we had quite given up hope of having a family. And now that she's going to Austria to stay with my sister for the summer, and then on to college in Switzerland, well, you see, we don't feel we can look after

Muffin. Elizabeth does it all, when she's here, and, to be honest, neither of us is very good with ponies."

"I know Jess will look after him, Mrs Carter, it's just the expense at the moment . . ."

"Oh, my dear, I quite understand," Mrs Carter interrupted, "but you needn't worry about that. We always buy Muffin's hay every year from the farm next door, so we'll have it sent over to you." She turned to Jess. "And when he needs shoeing, just tell Mr Croxford to send the bill to us – he's at Upper Edgecombe, you know."

And so it had all been arranged. The next morning, on his way to work, Dad had given Jess a lift over to the Carters' house, and she had ridden Muffin home.

Riding Muffin was a very different experience from being astride Beetle's broad back, as Jess soon discovered. To begin with, he was much smaller than Beetle. He was twelve hands high – too small for Jess, really, whereas Beetle was a little too big. But it was the different gait that Jess found so difficult to get used to. At the riding stable at Catley, Jess had been used to riding ponies of about Beetle's size, or slightly smaller, and she had grown used to the longer stride of a larger pony. As she bounced along on Muffin's back, rising to the trot at twice the normal rate, she wanted to laugh out loud. He was very sweet, though, she decided. His little ears were pricked and he held his head well, looking about him with interest. His long, thick, dark mane seemed to go all ways at once, falling on either side of his neck, and sticking up untidily between his ears. Despite his smallness, he was strongly built, and once Jess had learned to rise on every other stride of Muffin's trot, she began to enjoy riding the little chestnut pony.

Knowing Beetle's somewhat unpredictable nature, Jess had been a little concerned in case he did not take kindly to another pony sharing his orchard. However, she need not have worried. After a sniff and a squeal, the two ponies had settled down together quite amicably.

Now, Jess gazed thoughtfully at her two ponies. No – not *her* ponies, she reminded herself. She thought of her dream pony. Would he always remain a dream, she wondered. Her imagination conjured him up in the orchard at Trumpeter Cottage – her beautiful grey arab, with his banner tail and his exquisite, finely chiselled head. Always, when he saw her, he threw his nose in the air, tossed his long silken mane, whinnied that shrill call of welcome . . .

Seven

The Easter holidays were the busiest and the best that Jess had ever known. With two ponies to ride and look after, as well as the ginger kitten to feed, the time flew by, and soon school began again.

Taking Rachel's advice, Jess looked out for the poster at Edgecombe Post Office. When it duly appeared in the window, she discovered that entries for the show and gymkhana events could be made on the day. However, she sent for the schedule and studied the list of events.

Outside the little stone stable, Jess sat on an upturned bucket and chewed on a piece of grass, meditatively.

"Open Jumping, 14.2 hands and under . . . no jump over three foot six inches. I'm sure we could do it, Bee, if only you'd behave yourself." Jess looked towards the dark bay pony as he dozed in the sunshine. She had just given him a thorough grooming and she looked with pride at his shining coat. From outside the shed next to the stable, Muffin watched with bright, intelligent eyes, awaiting his turn to be groomed.

From his usual position, sitting on the warm flagstones, Tommy was arranging an assortment of cardboard boxes to form garages for his cars. He studied Muffin for a moment and then turned his blue eyes on Jess. "Can I ride Muffin?" he asked, unceremoniously.

"Well, you can't really *ride* him," Jess explained. "You haven't got a hard hat, you see, and mine would be too big for you." Then, seeing Tommy's crestfallen face, she added, "But I can sit you on his back. Come on, up you go!"

"But he *loves* it, Mum!"

"No, Jess, he's far too young."

Jess was sitting in the kitchen, feeding the ginger kitten. Suddenly she turned her attention from pleading for her young brother to be allowed to ride Muffin. "Oh look, Mum, his eyes are open!"

Mrs Caswell laughed. "Jess, I can't keep up with you! I presume you don't mean Tommy!" she chuckled, drying her hands and coming over to inspect the kitten, now named Dandelion by Jess, in view of his golden colour. "We're lucky to have reared him," she said. "What lovely blue eyes. I'm sure Tabitha and Tippy haven't opened theirs yet." While Mrs Caswell inspected the tabby kittens in their box, Jess cuddled the ginger kitten.

"Mum . . ."

"Yes, dear?"

"I *can* keep Dandy, can't I – he can be mine?"

Mrs Caswell smiled at her shy eldest daughter, who found it so difficult to make friends. "Of course you can, Jess," she said, "I can't make you find homes for the kittens after you saved their lives, can I?" She put an arm round her. "And you do very much want that pony, too, don't you? Don't despair, love – one of these days I'm sure it will happen. Beetle and Muffin are fine, but they're not the same as having a pony of your own to love, are they?"

Jess grinned back at her mother. "You know me too well," she said. "But I'm terribly lucky to have them, aren't I? Especially without having to pay for their keep. I'm going to enjoy them whilst I've got them."

"And you never know what's round the corner," added Mrs Caswell.

Mum had been right, Jess thought gloomily, as she watched the vet's van disappear down the lane in a cloud of dust. You never *do* know what's round the corner – maybe trouble!

It was the evening before the Upper Edge-combe show. That morning, just a week before he was due to return to his rightful owner, Beetle had gone suddenly and unaccountably lame.

"Can't tell you what might have caused it," the vet had said. "Difficult to say, really. I don't think it's anything to do with the jumping." Again, he ran his hand slowly and carefully down the leg. "There's no swelling, and no heat." Straightening up, he gave Beetle a pat on the neck. "Just rest, I think, old fellow," he said. Turning to Jess, he added, "I'm afraid the show tomorrow is out. Sorry about that, but we can't take any chances, can we?"

So next morning it was Muffin who stood outside the stone stable whilst Jess, assisted by Tommy, groomed him thoroughly.

"That bit you've done is very good, Tommy," Jess encouraged.

Tommy beamed with pleasure as he paused in his grooming of one of Muffin's legs. The lower part of Muffin's shoulder was as far as Tommy could reach. "Mum's going to take us to the show after dinner," he told Jess.

"You'll enjoy that, Tommy – there'll be lots of other ponies there."

Doggedly, Tommy set to work again, while Jess fetched the tack. Jess was determined not to let her disappointment spoil the day. She and Muffin were going to have fun!

As Jess drifted off to sleep that night, she thought of the day at the show. Muffin had enjoyed himself immensely, and so had Jess. The noise and fun and excitement of the show had affected them both. Jess thought of the showground – horse-boxes and cars packing the field, the blare of loudspeakers, and the whinnies and grunts of ponies as they moved excitedly about the ground. She and Muffin had entered several gymkhana events, and had even managed to win a rosette in the trotting race, much to Jess's amazement. Muffin had out-trotted ponies much larger than himself to finish in third place in the final heat. Jess was sure that he had held his head higher after she had tied the rosette to his bridle.

But a happening in the day which had only lasted for a few minutes was still vivid and fresh in Jess's mind, and eclipsed all other thoughts. She and Muffin had arrived at the show at lunchtime, in plenty of time for the gymkhana events. The showing classes were still taking place, but most of them were over, and some of the ponies were being boxed. Even as Jess trotted Muffin up the lane towards the showground entrance, horse-boxes were lumbering out of the wide gateway and heading for home, their occupants having already competed in their classes.

Jess, conscious of her long legs astride such a small pony, walked Muffin next to the hedge, keeping away from the main body of the show. As they passed by a row of large and luxurious horse-boxes, Jess suddenly halted Muffin and gazed in fascination. It was him! It really *was* – her dream pony! As Jess watched, her legs dangling on either side of Muffin's fat stomach, her dream pony pranced across her path, head held high. A girl of about Jess's age led the pony, which tossed its beautiful arab head and whinnied excitedly.

"Hey! Polly – steady now," said the girl, smiling at the pony and reaching up to smooth its elegant dapple-grey neck. The pony pushed her beautiful nose against the girl's arm and danced excitedly beside her, like a beautiful silver leaf floating in the breeze, Jess thought. Jess was transfixed. The pony was even more beautiful than she had imagined. Its head was so finely moulded, she could have imagined that it was made of china. Its long, dark grey mane was fine and silky, and moved beautifully on the pony's elegant neck as it pranced. Jess watched in fascination as the pony was led up the ramp of one of the horse-boxes, its long banner tail swishing in the interior of the box as the girl lifted the ramp and fastened the bolts.

In a trance, Jess heard the engine start up – the driver must have been at the wheel already. The girl climbed into the passenger side of the Land-Rover which pulled the box, and the horse-box moved off, bouncing gently over the uneven ground. Slowly, but surely, her dream pony moved away across the field and out of Jess's life. As the end of the box disappeared from sight, Jess awoke from her

47

soporific state, realising what an idiot she had been! Why, she asked herself crossly, as she and Muffin continued on their way, had she not *done* anything? Why hadn't she spoken to the girl – she had looked friendly enough. Jess's imagination took hold of her, as she saw herself talking to the girl, patting the dream pony's neck, and making an instant friend of the girl who then asked her back to tea. Here, Jess's imagination forgot Muffin's existence completely, as she stepped into the Land-Rover and travelled home with the girl, where she was offered a ride on the dream pony. It was as she jumped the four-foot gate, astride the beautiful arab, and watched admiringly by the girl, that Jess came back to earth with a bump – literally! Muffin, ambling along the grass path, ridden by a daydreamer who was paying him no attention, stopped suddenly and unexpectedly, and put his head down to graze. Jess found herself sliding down his neck to a sitting position next to his nose.

Muffin eyed her, mildly, and continued to pull at the grass. Just for a second, before she began to laugh, and as she looked up at the fat little pony, Jess felt an overwhelming sense of despair. Little Muffin was sweet, and Beetle was lovely, too, in his own way, but would she *ever* have her dream pony? Her desire for her own pony was as strong and as desperate as ever. She knew how lucky she was to be able to ride other people's ponies, but how she longed for one of her own – especially her dream pony. And she had seen him – or, more exactly, *her*. Her dream pony was called Polly – but she belonged to someone else. Jess heaved a large sigh of self-pity. All the ponies in the world seemed to belong to someone else . . .

"What are you doing *there*, Dess?"

Tommy, gazing down at her from his wide-open blue eyes, brought her sense of humour back to her.

"Being a hopeless rider!" Jess laughed, getting up and brushing herself down. Then Clare and Kim appeared, closely followed by Mum.

During the rest of the day, Jess's mind kept returning to Polly, the beautiful arab pony, but she tried hard to push these thoughts from her. Jess told herself, firmly, that her dream pony must remain as it had always been – a pony of her dreams. Reality was Muffin, tired but jogging happily home to his well-earned bucket of food.

It was when Muffin had been reunited with Beetle in the orchard, and Jess had taken herself wearily to bed, that she allowed herself to think again of the arab pony. After all, she *was* her dream pony, Jess thought. Through sleep-blurred eyes, Jess looked at her china horse and remembered Polly's beautiful china-like head, and the dark grey forelock which spread in wisps about

49

her large eyes. Was it her imagination, or did the china horse's head turn towards her? Polly and the china horse then merged into one beautiful grey arab pony which cantered through Jess's dreams that night.

Eight

The summer was long, glorious and very hot. Day after day, the sun shone from a cloudless sky. As the weeks and months passed, the green of the countryside paled and turned to brown. The orchard at Trumpeter Cottage became a lifeless desert, as the old apple trees searched out the last moisture from the ground.

Beetle's lameness had disappeared after a week's rest, and he had returned to Rachel in June. Soon, the grass in the orchard was non-existent, and Muffin stood forlornly in the dusty brown field. Much to Jess's relief, the promised hay arrived for Muffin in mid-July, and she began feeding him straight away. She rode round to see Mrs Carter to explain.

"I know he still looks well," Jess said, "but he's lost quite a lot of weight already and there just isn't any grass – he's really hungry!"

Mrs Carter stroked Muffin's neck gingerly. She was nervous of ponies and approached little Muffin with slight trepidation. "Of course you must feed him," she agreed. "You can't deny Muffin his food," she added, laughing. "It's the most important thing in life to him!"

As the summer progressed, restrictions were put on the use of water in the home, and the use of garden hoses and sprinklers was forbidden as the drought continued. The garden at Trumpeter Cottage, which Mum had tended so carefully throughout the spring, gradually shrivelled to a state of brown hibernation. Nothing grew, as some plants conserved energy, and others withered and died. The stream at the back of the cottage dried up, and Jess carried water to the orchard every day.

"It's typical!" said Dad one Saturday morning, pausing on his way through the kitchen, laden with pots of paint and brushes. "As soon as I finish the bathroom, we can't use it!"

Mum turned from the kitchen dresser. "Well, I did think that we might have a bath this evening," she suggested, tentatively.

"Can I have it first?" asked Kim, promptly.

"Oh, Mum, *that's* not fair," wailed Clare. "She had it first last time. I *hate* having someone else's bathwater!"

"Nobody *likes* having dirty bathwater," Kim retorted, "but if we're not supposed to use very much water, what else can we do? I don't really *want* a bath," she added, plaintively, to Mum.

"No arguing," said Mum, firmly. "It'll be Tommy first, anyway, since he goes to bed before the rest of you. We can't waste the water – at least one of you must use it after him." She sighed. "Oh, won't it be lovely when we have some rain . . ."

When it finally arrived, on the last day of the summer holidays, the rain came with a vengeance. All day, the sky darkened, and thunder rolled around the hills. At last, after tea, the first drops began to fall. The four Caswell children rushed out into the garden, followed by their parents.

"It's lovely! It's lovely!" Tommy cried, jumping up and down on the lifeless brown lawn, and holding out his chubby hands in an effort to catch the drops of rain as they fell. The girls, too, danced and shrieked with delight as the rain quickly soaked their hair and clothes.

"Come on in, you idiots!" laughed Mum, running back into the cottage. The rain was lashing down now, crackling against the dry, brittle leaves of the trees.

Jess stopped her dance of delight. "Look!" she panted, pointing towards the kitchen door. "Look at the kittens – they don't know what the rain is!"

Standing in line in the doorway, the two tabbies and Dandy were gazing out, wide-eyed. They crouched down, and Dandy hissed as the rain lashed down on the stone step and bounced off it into their faces. Jess ran back and picked up Dandy, hugging him. "It's rain, Dandy – real, lovely, wet rain!" she told him delightedly. "Now Muffin's water trough will fill up, and the flowers can grow again – and the grass!"

But Dandy was not too sure about it. For ten minutes, he and his two sisters sat by the kitchen stove, licking their paws and washing the strange wetness off their fur.

With the coming of the rain, the temperature dropped to autumn coolness. On the first day of term, Jess was quite glad to be wearing her new school winter clothes. It was strange to be putting on a skirt, socks and a blouse, after so many weeks of shorts and T-shirts, but Jess shivered in the unaccustomed chilliness of the September morning. Or maybe she was shivering with fright! Jess brushed her hair in front of the mirror in the bathroom, from where her own grey eyes looked back at her in trepidation. Goodness, she told herself, it was only a new school that she was going to – not a prison! It was such a large comprehensive – that was the trouble – and Jess would know very few people. Still, she reminded herself, Rachel would be there, somewhere, and there would be other faces she knew.

"Are you ready, Jess? We mustn't be late!" Dad called up the stairs, and soon the rush of getting away pushed all nervous thoughts from Jess's mind.

Kim, Clare and Tommy were still eating a leisurely breakfast in the kitchen, when Jess rushed through the hall, gathering up her anorak and her school bag on the way.

" 'Bye, kids," Jess called, grinning in through the kitchen doorway at her younger siblings.

Clare looked mildly offended, whilst Kim wrinkled her nose. " 'Bye, big sister!" she mocked. "Don't get too lost in the big school!" Tommy turned his serious blue eyes towards Jess. "I'll look after Muffin for you," he stated importantly.

Jess laughed. "I *will* be coming home again, Tommy," she called, stopping to stroke Dandy, who had followed her downstairs and was balancing on the dresser, playing with the strap of her bag with his paw.

"Off you go!" commanded Mum, sweeping her out through the front door. "You don't want to be late on your first day." She smiled at her eldest daughter, knowing how nervous she was feeling. "Enjoy yourself, love, and don't worry – it'll take a while to get used to everything."

It was a dismal, grey morning. As Dad drove the car along the lane towards the motorway, he switched on the heater and the radio.

"We'll pretend it's still summer in here," he said, turning to smile at Jess. "This weather will take a bit of getting used to, after the lovely summer."

"Mmm." With time to think, Jess was beginning to worry again. While Dad hummed to the music on the radio, Jess huddled nervously in her seat. They turned on to the motorway, and Dad switched on the car lights, since the sky had darkened and rain was falling steadily. Jess rubbed at the steamed-up window and peered out, watching the countryside flashing by.

It was then that she saw the pony. It was just a lightish shape, standing miserably by a gate, but something about it caught at Jess's heart. There was something wrong with that pony, she was sure. Jess rubbed the window again and strained to look, but pony, field and gate had sped by. Jess caught sight of a village near the motorway.

"What's that village called, Dad?" she asked.

"Oh – I think that's Currington Brayley," Dad replied.

"I didn't recognise it from the motorway." Jess's mind was busy working it out. The pony wasn't too far away from Trumpeter Cottage. The route to the motorway from the cottage curved round and away from the direction of the comprehensive school, so that after the car had joined the motorway, it had actually passed by the cottage and Edgecombe on the way. Currington Brayley was the next village along the valley after Lower Edgecombe, so the pony must be in a field somewhere between Lower Edgecombe and Currington Brayley.

Jess knew that she must find that pony. Even though she had only seen it for a short moment, she knew that something was wrong, although she could not explain to herself exactly what it was.

All through her day at the new school, Jess thought of the pony, and planned her visit. She saw Rachel, briefly, but only had time to hear about the visit to America and enquire after Beetle's lameness.

"Oh, I think he just decided to have a rest," Rachel laughed. "He was perfectly OK when he got home."

The day at the comprehensive school passed slowly, but was not as awe-inspiring as Jess had anticipated. She even found that some other members of her year felt as nervous as she did in this new and much larger environment. At the end of the school day, Jess caught the bus home. She sat restlessly in the bus as it slowly rattled its way around the twisting country lanes. The driver seemed to be in no great hurry, and he chatted cheerfully to each new passenger who arrived. At last, the bus eased to a halt by the ancient oak tree at Edgecombe Post Office.

"Enjoy your first day?" asked the driver, as Jess dismounted.

Jess smiled. Everyone knew everything about everyone else in the country! "Yes thanks," she replied.

The rain had stopped during the afternoon, but the sky was still overcast. Jess hurried up the lane to Trumpeter Cottage. Sitting on the gatepost, his tail curving round the post, was Dandy. He meowed his greeting when he saw Jess, and climbed into her arms to be cuddled when she reached the gate.

"Hello, little Dandy," she crooned, "have you missed me?" On her way up the path, Jess told Dandy about the pony, and she told Mum, too, as she hurried upstairs to change. There was Muffin to see, and Tommy, who followed her, questioning her constantly about the day at school, but at last Jess was away astride her bicycle.

It wasn't too difficult to work out approximately where the pony's field was situated. Within twenty minutes, Jess was in the area, and then followed a field-by-field search. At the fourth gate, Jess stopped, dispirited. Surely, she hadn't made a mistake? Perhaps the pony had been taken away . . . But no, there it was! As Jess stared again at the pony, this time from a closer proximity, her heart turned over – and then over again! Not only did the pony look miserable, neglected and in trouble, but also, unless Jess was very much mistaken, it was her dream pony – Polly, the beautiful grey arab!

Nine

"Polly! Hello, Polly!" Jess called, and the pony turned her head wearily. Climbing the gate, Jess approached the pony. Tears stung her eyes as she remembered the beautiful pony that had danced across her path at Upper Edgecombe Horse Show. Jess remembered how she had thought, then, that Polly seemed like a beautiful silver leaf, dancing in the wind. Her heart ached, now, when she saw how wearily Polly moved, and how dull were the large, dark eyes which turned to look at her as she approached. The pony's fine coat, still wet from the day's rain, clung to her body, accentuating her thinness. Jess noticed how awkwardly Polly was standing next to the water trough. As she came closer to the pony, she could see the reason.

Over a period of months, Polly's hooves had grown, and her shoes, firmly and well fitted by the blacksmith, had stayed in position. As a result, the growing feet had split, and formed into awkward shapes, restricted as they were by the farrier's nails and the iron shoes. Polly was now only able to move about awkwardly and painfully.

The ache in Jess's heart turned to anger. How *could* the girl who owned this beautiful pony have treated her in this way? It was obvious from looking at the state of the field, and at Polly's thinness, that she had not been fed during the drought. Hot tears of anger and frustration fell on Jess's cheeks. What could she *do*? Running back to her bicycle, Jess pulled out the bag of carrots she had brought, and hurried over to give them to the pony, who crunched them up greedily. Jess thought quickly. She must cycle home and return before dark with as much hay as she could manage on her bike – or maybe Mum would give her a lift in the car. Then, she must find out where the girl who owned Polly lived, and tell her of the arab pony's distress. Again, anger welled up inside Jess as she thought of the needless suffering that Polly was enduring, through her owner's thoughtlessness. And yet, Jess thought, the girl she had seen had not seemed like that. She had appeared to love Polly . . . it was puzzling.

Her mind full of these thoughts, Jess allowed herself a moment to smooth the dappled neck and to whisper in one of Polly's small, pointed ears, "I'll be back, girlie – don't you worry. You shall have some food soon." She imagined that she could see a spark of hope in those dark, liquid eyes. As she reached up to give Polly a final pat, a voice called out:

"I say!"

Jess swung round to see a man and a woman standing by the gate. The man waved a hand and called out again.

"Do you think you could just check the water in the trough for us, please? It would save us coming through the mud."

Casting a cursory glance in the direction of the trough, which contained a plentiful supply of water, Jess left Polly and walked across to the gate. They must be her parents, she thought, seething with anger. She can't be bothered to come herself, and they're too lazy to walk across the field!

Jess reached the gate. "There is plenty of water," she told them coldly. She took a breath, ready to tell them, urgently, how cruelly and thoughtlessly the pony had been treated – but the woman spoke first.

"Thank you *so* much, dear." She smiled at Jess, but her eyes looked worn out and defeated. Jess hesitated, and the woman continued. "We are in a hurry, you see, to visit our daughter. She's in hospital – we just came to see that her pony is all right. We have checked her water all through the drought, but now I expect, with the rain, we shan't have to come."

All at once, Jess understood, and her anger vanished.

"Oh . . . oh, I see . . . I'm sorry," she stammered. Then she spoke again, the words pouring out and tumbling over each other. "But, you see, your daughter's pony *isn't* all right. She's starving. And her feet are in a terrible state – she can hardly walk. She needs food and a blacksmith – urgently!"

The two stared at Jess blankly, and Jess had the feeling that this was just one more problem to add to their already problem-strewn life. "But . . . but, we had no idea—" the man began.

"It's all right," Jess said, quickly, "please don't worry. I can help – if you'd like me to. I've got some hay at home. I can bring her some. But she really *does* need the blacksmith. I think she's very uncomfortable – her feet are in a bad state."

The man turned to his wife. "But this is terrible, Maisie," he said to her. "Beckie thinks we are looking after her pony – but we seem to have neglected it, without realising." He turned back towards Jess. "We would be very grateful, young lady, if you *could* help," he told her, quietly. "Should we have fed the pony – in the *summer*?"

Jess nodded. "There's been no grass," she explained, "and now there will be just mud for a while."

"How stupid of us," the woman contributed. "We thought that water was the only thing to worry about in the drought, you see . . . and the blacksmith – well, Beckie always sees to that . . ."

The man looked at his watch, "Now, look – er, I'm afraid we don't know your name—"

"Jess Caswell – I live at Edgecombe, in Trumpeter Cottage, just down the lane from Edgecombe Farm."

"Well, Jess, if you could help us, we would be most grateful. We have to go to the hospital now." His eyes clouded with pain as he explained. "She's very ill, you see, so we must go. If you *could* give the pony some hay, and arrange for the blacksmith to come, we will call round to see you – you mustn't be out of pocket." He shook her hand. "Thank you very much, Jess. We'll see you again – oh, by the way, we live at Horwood House in Currington Brayley – Stockwood's the name."

That night, Jess lay in bed, unable to sleep. Questions and thoughts kept forming in her mind. How was Polly now, in her muddy, grassless field by the motorway? Would the blacksmith be able to come tomorrow? After she had taken some hay to Polly in her field, Jess had left a message with the blacksmith's wife, explaining the urgency, and asking if he could possibly call at the field on the following evening, after schooltime.

Then Jess's mind turned to the Stockwoods. How ill was Beckie Stockwood, she wondered sleepily, remembering the girl who had smiled up at her beautiful arab pony with such delight at the horse show. As she drifted off to sleep, Jess's last question was would Mr and Mrs Stockwood let her look after Polly while their daughter was ill? There was room in the orchard with Muffin. And, maybe, when Polly's feet had been attended to and when, with some food inside her, she had picked up, maybe . . . just maybe, they would let Jess ride her . . .

Jess yawned, stretching down her hand to stroke Dandy, who was curled in a tight ball on the duvet, next to her legs. Sleepily, Dandy opened his yellow eyes and purred.

"That would be so lovely, Dandy," Jess murmured, already half asleep, "to ride Polly . . ."

Ten

"Well, I don't know, I'm sure!"

Stan Croxford, the blacksmith from Upper Edgecombe, looked askance at Jess as he lifted out his portable anvil from a battered old van, and then reached in again for the butane burner. He straightened up and looked at Jess, thoughtfully.

"I don't know what your secret is, Jess Caswell, but today was the *third* time in less than six months that I've been telephoned by an owner, saying that *he* will pay for the shoeing of a pony that *you* are looking after!"

"I'm only helping out with this one," Jess admitted, smoothing Polly's thin neck, "but I'd love to look after her properly."

Again, Stan Croxford reached into his elderly vehicle, this time producing a bag of tools. "Is that so?" he said, grinning. "Well, Mr Stockwood gave me to understand that you might be looking after Polly for a while – said any attention needed would be paid for by him."

Jess held Polly, while Stan lifted the pony's front foot and began pulling out the nails in the old shoe. "What I'd *really* like," Jess confided, "is to keep her in the orchard at the cottage, with Muffin – you know, the pony you shod last month—"

"I know," Stan chuckled, "another one!" Carefully, he trimmed Polly's broken hoof. "You specialise in other people's ponies, do you?" he asked, releasing his hold on the hoof and straightening up again.

"I'm afraid so," Jess admitted, sadly.

"Never had one of your own?"

She shook her head.

Stan moved round to the other front leg. "Never mind," he said cheerily. "You'll have it one day – if you really want one. I was twenty-four before I had my old Major . . ."

For the next three-quarters of an hour, Jess listened to Stan Croxford's adventures with his sixteen-hand cob, whilst inside her mind an excited hope tingled. Would she, perhaps, be allowed to look after this beautiful pony?

While her feet were cut back to shape and new shoes were fitted, Polly stood, pulling at the hay in a net which Jess had brought over on her bike.

"There we are, then," said Stan, at last, stepping back to admire his work. "That's a good job, if I do say it myself. You look much more comfortable now, Polly," he told the arab pony. "A bit of food inside her – pony nuts and such like," he said, turning to Jess, "and she'll be as right as rain in no time. Surprising how

hardy these arabs are, you know, despite their light build."

Jess leaned on the gate, watching Polly pull at the hay, and admiring the light build that Stan had referred to. Of course, Polly was very thin now, but after some feeding . . .

The sound of a vehicle coming to a halt in the lane disturbed Jess's thoughts. She turned to see the front end of a Land-Rover. Emerging from the doors were Mr and Mrs Stockwood and then, much to Jess's surprise, her father appeared on the scene.

"Dad! Whatever are *you* doing here?"

He grinned at her. "Any excuse to get out of the decorating," he said, winking.

"Jess, we've come to ask you a favour," said Mr Stockwood. "Your parents say that they don't mind and they think that you won't, either."

Jess looked at him with a puzzled expression on her face. Then Mrs Stockwood stepped forward.

"Jess, dear, would you do us a big favour – would you look after Polly at your home, while Beckie is in hospital? Keep her in your orchard and feed her – ride her if you would like to." She paused. *"Please*, Jess, it will be such a relief to us to know that she is being looked after."

Jess gazed at them in amazement. She heard Stan Croxford chuckling as he loaded the equipment into his van.

At last, Jess found her voice. *"Like* to?" she questioned, incredulously, "but I'd *love* to!"

At Trumpeter Cottage, Jess felt as though she were part of one of her own dreams, as she led Polly down the ramp of the horse-box into the lane. With comfortable shoes fitted and some hay inside her, Polly seemed to have regained some of her former spirit. She viewed her new surroundings with interest, tossing her beautiful head and even jogging on the spot beside Jess.

"She's beautiful, isn't she?" said Mum, who had come out to see the new arrival, accompanied by the rest of the family, including Badger and the three kittens. Muffin, hearing the sound of Polly's shoes clattering on the road, whinnied from the orchard, and received a return call from Polly.

"What a large family you have!" laughed Mrs Stockwood. "I'm sure Polly will like it here."

Still feeling slightly unreal, Jess led Polly down the drive, past the old stone stable to the orchard, where a very curious Muffin was waiting at the gate.

Later on, after a quick tea, Jess sat on the orchard gate, watching the two ponies eating their hay from the net, which Jess had hung from one of the old apple trees. Watching Polly's grey shape soften into the dusk, Jess remembered Stan Croxford's words: "You specialise in other people's ponies, do you?" he had asked.

Jess sighed. Never mind, she thought, as Polly turned her head to gaze at Jess out of the darkness, just for now, at least, my dream pony really *is* here in the orchard!

"Polly," she called, softly, and out of the dark came a gentle answering whicker. Then the back door of Trumpeter Cottage opened, throwing out light on to the path.

"Jess!" Mum called, "are you coming in, or shall I bring out a tent for you!"

Jess slid down from the gate. "Goodnight – other people's ponies," she called, but this time her only reply was the steady munching of hay from the night-filled orchard.

Eleven

Mr Warburton, the vet, came over to Trumpeter Cottage to give Polly a check-up, having been sent by Mr Stockwood.

"Basically, she's reasonably fit," he confirmed cheerfully. "Lucky you caught her in time, though," he added. "She just needs nutrition." He took a syringe from his bag. "I'll give her a vitamin injection," he told Jess, "and I'll give you some powder to mix in her food."

That afternoon, a delivery of pony nuts, crushed oats, bran and flaked maize arrived from the Corn Stores in Currington Brayley.

"All paid for by Mr Stockwood of Horwood House," the delivery man said, as he carried each sack down the path of Trumpeter Cottage, and deposited it in the stone shed next to the stable. "I've arranged for some hay and straw to be sent over to you early next week," he added.

After the delivery van had driven away, creaking carefully around the curving lane, Jess gazed thoughtfully at the bulging hessian sacks. In true cat fashion, the three kittens were investigating these new arrivals. Dandy, always the leader, was

71

the first to climb one of the sacks, and survey the world of the shed from its top.

Jess began feeding Polly straight away, giving her a small feed twice a day, to begin with, as instructed by the vet, and she continued to put out hay for both the ponies. After only a week, the difference in the grey arab was noticeable, and at the weekend Jess decided to ride Polly for the first time.

"I'll ride you this afternoon," Jess promised Muffin, who stood disconsolately at the gate, as Jess led Polly towards the stable. The grey pony danced beside her excitedly.

"You know you're going for a ride, don't you?" Jess said, as she brushed Polly lightly. All that week, Jess had groomed the grey mare thoroughly, each evening after school, and now her coat shone like silk.

"I wonder when you were ridden last," Jess mused. "Perhaps it was the show at Upper Edgecombe." As she saddled the grey arab, Jess found herself thinking about Beckie Stockwood. What had happened to her, she wondered, and how was she now? How long would it be before she could ride again?

"You know, Polly," Jess said, as she tightened the girth, "I think I'll write to her."

Jess found her hands trembling with excitement as she gathered up the reins and prepared to mount. She could feel excitement tingling through Polly, too. Jess jumped into the saddle and at last she was astride her beautiful dream pony! Feeling again as though she were back in one of her dreams, Jess felt Polly's light, quick movements as they started off down the path and into the lane.

"She feels wonderful!"

Jess's eyes shone as she described her first ride on Polly to Clare and Kim.

"She must feel terribly different from Muffin," Clare observed. Clare sat on one side of the fireplace, drawing the kittens, who were asleep on the rug, whilst Kim sat cross-legged on the other side, frowning and chewing her pencil over her English homework.

Trumpeter Cottage boasted a large lounge, but invariably the family congregated either in the big, square kitchen, warmed by the old range, or – where the girls now were – in the cosy living room, which led from the kitchen and which also served as a dining room. When not in use, the dining table was pushed against the window, and the big, comfortable chairs formed a semi-circle in front of the fire.

A standard lamp and the bright log fire lit the room, and purple shadows danced and fell on the walls at the whim of the flames. Outside, on this particular night, the weather was wild, wet and windy. An easterly wind shook the windows, and tugged at the ivy which grew over the outside walls, lifting it and throwing it back, so that the long tendrils scratched and tapped against the window panes like the claws of some large and desperate animal.

"She's gorgeous," Jess told Clare dreamily. "It's like riding on a cloud – she's so light and . . . sort of . . . delicate."

Kim looked up. "I wish *you* could write my composition homework," she said, plaintively. "I'm just no good at English – I've got to write about 'A sunny day at the weekend'."

"Well, that's easy," Jess replied, "I'll describe what it's like going for a ride on Polly and you can write it down. After all, it doesn't say it has to be about what *you* do." Kim looked doubtful.

"You can add some bits about you, too," Jess encouraged, warming to the idea, "then it will be your own work. It's not cheating – just getting a helping hand! I'm going to write to Beckie, anyway, and I'll describe riding Polly to her."

"Who's Beckie?"

"Beckie Stockwood. She's the girl who owns Polly. She must feel terribly fed up with not being able to ride. I thought it might cheer her up."

Jess posted the letter the next day, addressing it to Horwood House, and enclosing with it a drawing of the kittens asleep by the fire, and another one of Polly's head. Towards the end of the following week, a letter arrived for Jess, postmarked from Bristol. It was evening before Jess received it, since she had to leave for school each morning before the post arrived.

Hanging her anorak in the hall, and extracting a piece of chocolate cake from the tin in the kitchen, Jess made her way to the living room, opening the letter as she went. Clare and Kim were already ensconced in their favourite places by the fire. Clare was reading and Kim sighing over her homework.

"Not English again?" Jess mumbled, through the chocolate cake.

"No, Maths this time," Kim replied, glumly. Looking up, she added, more cheerfully, "I got an A for the composition about you and Polly." She grinned up at Jess, "Mrs Bloxton said I'd made a dramatic improvement!"

"Mm . . ." Jess was lost to all thoughts of Kim's miraculous change with her English work, as she read the long letter from Beckie Stockwood.

"Dear Jess," the letter began. "It was lovely to receive your letter last week. Sorry I've been so long in replying, but I have had pneumonia, following an operation, and I didn't feel much like writing – or doing anything! Actually, I can't remember much about the last two weeks – I think I was quite ill and Mum and Dad were worried. Anyway, I'm better now, and they have told me all about you. Thank you, *thank you* for looking after Polly for me . . ."

Jess sat cross-legged on the hearth-rug next to the kittens, and leaned against one of the armchairs as she continued to read the letter. Beckie told of the car accident which had sent her into hospital in Bristol as an emergency. It had been in June when the accident happened. Beckie had been driven by her mother to the outskirts of Bristol for her weekly flute lesson. On the way home, another car had driven through the traffic lights at a junction, crashing into their car on Beckie's side. Mrs Stockwood had received only minor cuts and bruises, but Beckie had been rushed to hospital.

"I can't remember anything about that day," Beckie wrote, "or for quite a time afterwards. And since then I seem to have had nothing but operations. Still, things are looking a little more hopeful now. The nurses are even talking about 'when you go home'! I don't think it will be for quite a while, though, so I *really* am grateful to you – especially for discovering Polly's condition when you did. I kept asking Mum and Dad if she was all right, and of course they thought all they had to worry about was water, with the drought we've had. Never mind, it's all water under the bridge – if you'll pardon the pun!"

The letter was cheerful and optimistic, and finished, "Please, *please* do write again. It was so lovely to hear about Polly. Please tell me about you, too – and your family and pets. I've got no brothers or sisters, and only Polly as a pet, so I'm rather boring! Still, Polly makes up for everything – she's such a sweet pony, isn't she? I love the drawings you sent. I miss Polly so much – I can't wait to get home and ride her. Perhaps we could ride together? *Please* write. Love, Beckie.

PS Enclosed is a drawing of the garden here. It's not a very exciting subject, but there's not much else to draw except the other patients – and the nurses, of course, but *they* don't stay still for long enough! It was a nice day today, so the nurses let me sit outside."

"Gosh, *that*'s good," Kim exclaimed as Jess held the drawing up for inspection. "Did Beckie do it?"

Twelve

Letters began to fly back and forth between Trumpeter Cottage and the hospital in Bristol. Sometimes Mr and Mrs Stockwood arrived at the cottage, bearing Beckie's fat envelope.

"You're working wonders," Mrs Stockwood told Jess, on one of their visits. "Beckie has improved such a lot since you began writing to her. She was getting depressed with being in hospital for so long – thought she'd *never* come out!"

"Well, we began to think so, too, didn't we, Maisie?" Mr Stockwood contributed.

"That's right. But now they say it won't be long before she will be home!"

Jess noticed that Mrs Stockwood's eyes had lost the strained, almost defeated look which she had observed when she first met Beckie's parents. Her eyes smiled at Jess, now, as she rested a hand on her shoulder.

"You've no idea how grateful we are, Jess," Mrs Stockwood told her.

"But ... but, I haven't done anything," Jess insisted. "It's wonderful being able to look after Polly – and I really enjoy writing to Beckie and getting her letters. We seem to . . . to, well, *think* the same about things . . ." Jess stopped, feeling suddenly embarrassed. She picked up Dandy and stroked him to hide her confusion.

"Well, you've taken a load off our minds, young lady, one way and another," said Mr Stockwood, in his deep, no-nonsense voice. "Our Beckie's a different girl since you came along."

Mum handed round tea and biscuits, and Jess was able to slip away to read Beckie's latest letter in the solitude of her bedroom. The letter was full of excitement.

"Doctor James has said that I'll be home for Christmas," Beckie wrote. "Won't that be wonderful! I seem to have been in here for ever!"

With each of Beckie's letters was enclosed a drawing, sometimes two. This time, it was a drawing of Sister Pye – "Old Crusty" as the nurses called her. "Actually," Beckie wrote, "she's very kind, but she doesn't like to show it. She struts around the ward all stiff and starchy, with her lips pursed, watching the nurses and pouncing on them if she thinks they're doing something wrong. But she's really great if you're in pain, or feeling miserable."

Jess paused in her reading. Beckie's letters were always cheerful. She didn't ever mention that she felt miserable, or depressed, but she must do . . .

"It's October now," the letter continued. "Just think, Jess, I might be home in two months – eight weeks! Oh, I'm getting excited already!"

Jess leaned back against the headboard of her bed and tried to imagine what it must be like to be in hospital and longing to be home with Polly. She looked out through her window and across to the orchard. She could just see two swishing tails – one black and one dark grey. She sighed. She must remember that her beautiful dream pony belonged to someone else and soon Polly must return to Beckie, who loved her. It was hard to have found your dream pony and then to know that she could never be yours . . .

Dandy had followed Jess upstairs. He jumped up on to the bed and rubbed himself against her, purring and kneading the duvet cover with his small ginger paws. Jess gathered him into her arms and hugged him.

"Never mind, Dandy. I've got you, haven't I?" Dandy's purrs grew even louder and his yellow eyes gazed adoringly at Jess. "Come on," said Jess, "let's go and see Polly. If I'm quick, I can ride to the woods and back before dark."

The evenings were drawing in. Next week, the clocks would go back, and there would be no time after school in which to ride. But if she got up early, perhaps she could ride in the extra hour . . . Her depression forgotten – or perhaps pushed to the back of her mind – Jess ran down the narrow cottagey stairs, two at a time, followed by Dandy, who skittered excitedly down the stairway, imagining intriguing animals to pounce upon at every turn.

The weeks seemed to fly by. As each day passed, Jess could not help thinking that it was another day less with Polly. She tried hard not to think about it, sharing her precious riding time between the two ponies. The steady flow of letters to and from Beckie continued. As October gave way to November, and then December arrived, Jess knew that the time was approaching when she must relinquish her part in Polly's care.

"But I'll always love you, Polly," she told the grey mare after school one evening in early December. "Beckie will let me come over to see you and ride you sometimes – she said so."

Jess heard the unmistakable sound of Tommy approaching through the dusk. Tommy's passion for ponies – and Muffin in particular – had increased over the months. Everywhere he went, he would click his tongue in an imitation of the sound of horses' hooves. When enquiries were made, he would explain that he was riding Muffin.

Mum was still insistent that Tommy was too young to ride. "You'll have to give in, Mum," Jess had told her that week, "to save his sanity!"

"But he's only four, Jess."

"Mum, lots of four year olds ride!"

Now, Tommy arrived, breathlessly tongue-clicking, at Jess's side.

"You can't be riding Muffin, Tommy," Jess informed him. "Muffin's there, in the orchard, eating his hay."

"'Course I'm not, silly," Tommy replied stoutly. "I'm riding Miffin!"

"And what's Miffin like?" Jess enquired, laughing.

"He's just like Muffin," Tommy stated unabashed. "He's his twin brother!"

Thirteen

The day had come at last. Jess had known that it must. She had expected to feel miserable at the prospect of losing Polly, and excited at the thought of meeting Beckie. But, somehow, she did not seem to feel *anything*.

It was Saturday. A pale sun shone in a cloudless sky, and the air was cold and crisp – one of those December days that are perfect for riding. But, for Jess, it might as well have been pouring with rain, for she could not enjoy the ride to Horwood House, a distance of about four miles along the beautiful Edgecombe Valley.

No member of the Caswell family had been able to extract many words from Jess that morning. She munched her way mechanically through her bowl of muesli, while Tommy chattered to her about Muffin. Eventually, even Tommy's cheery voice came to a faltering halt. At last, when Jess had groomed and saddled Polly, lingering over these chores for longer than usual, a subdued family gathered at the gate to say goodbye to Polly.

"I'm sure we shall see you again, Polly," said Mum, trying to sound cheerful. She smoothed the arab's silky, grey neck. Polly pushed her soft nose hopefully into Mum's hand and was not disappointed. As Polly crunched her carrot, Clare and Kim patted her. Tommy, standing a little apart, was unusually quiet.

"Aren't you going to say goodbye to Polly, Tom?" Dad asked. Tommy shook his head, his grey eyes brimming with tears. Tommy, although bright and cheerful, was very sensitive.

"I think I'd better go," Jess muttered. She squeezed Polly with her heels and the pony stepped away with her usual willingness. Soon, they were away from the cottage, swinging down the lane towards Currington Brayley.

Jess was quiet during the ride. Normally, she would chatter to Polly, watching those neat little arab ears flicking back to listen, and delighting in the lightness of Polly's step. But today a cloud of gloom had settled over Jess, leaving her feeling numb and empty, and she was glad when the village of Currington Brayley came into sight.

Beckie had sent instructions for how to find Horwood House, and had even drawn a map. Jess had looked at it so many times, and read the instructions over and over, that she knew the way by heart. Turn left at the first cross-roads after the 30-mile-an-hour sign, past the church, then second right. Horwood House was down the lane, just past Horwood Farm.

Jess and Polly had to wait whilst a herd of Friesian cows pattered across the road from the farm, and into the field opposite. A border collie darted from side to side, busily ensuring that his herd would not stray. Not that they looked in any danger of straying, Jess thought, as she watched the patient cows plodding slowly across the lane, lowered head to swishing tail. One cow *did* stop to stare. Her sisters kept swaying past – a gently flowing black and white river continuing on its way across the lane. The rebel cow turned large, curious eyes upon the newcomers.

Polly suddenly remembered her arab ancestry, and tossed her head and pointed her nose in the air. She whinnied shrilly and pawed the ground, then pranced and danced across the lane in mock fear. For the first time that morning, Jess laughed.

"You idiot!" she chuckled, stroking Polly's neck soothingly. "You're not a bit frightened, really – and you know it!"

The collie, full of importance, hurried to direct the cow, making the way clear for Jess and Polly to move on down the lane towards the gates of Horwood House.

Here it was, then! As Jess viewed the elegant, old, ivy-clad house, noting the block of stabling and outbuildings to one side at the back, she realised that this was the end of her short but happy relationship with Polly. This was Polly's home – where she lived for some of the year. Possibly she was stabled during the colder months of winter. Polly knew this house and driveway well – her head was held high, her ears pricked and she walked with an excited step.

As Jess kicked her feet out of the stirrups and slid down from the saddle, the misery which had remained dormant all morning suddenly came to the surface, taking her by surprise. Blinding tears leapt to Jess's eyes and chased each other down her cheeks. She flung her arms around Polly's neck and sobbed into the arab pony's dark mane. Polly stood very still, turning her beautiful head to nudge Jess's arm gently. Jess pulled a handkerchief from her anorak pocket, wiped her wet face and blew her nose. Polly snorted hopefully at the handkerchief and, despite her misery, Jess found herself laughing again.

"Trust you to think it's food!" she said, stroking Polly and smoothing the long strands of forelock which hung delicately about the brow-band. "Sorry about that, Polly," she continued. "I shouldn't be such a baby. I've brought you home to Beckie. You haven't seen Beckie for *ages* – and she's longing to see you. Come on!"

Allowing herself a large sniff and a further quick rub with the handkerchief, Jess resolutely led Polly towards the front door and rang the bell. Almost at once, the door was opened and there stood Mrs Stockwood, beaming with pleasure.

"Jess! You're here – how lovely! Would you like to take Polly round to the back. There's a ring outside the stable – you can tie her up there, if you will. Then I'll take you in to meet Beckie."

Jess led Polly round to the back of the house. As she replaced Polly's bridle with the head-collar, which she had secured to the pommel of the saddle before leaving Trumpeter Cottage, Jess found herself wondering how Beckie Stockwood was feeling. As she tied the rope to the ring in the wall, unfastened the girth and lifted the saddle from Polly's back, she wondered if she and Beckie would like each other as much as they had seemed to in their letters. Being reticent by nature, Jess tended to be wary of new relationships, and she felt nervous as she propped the saddle against the stable wall and hung the bridle from a convenient hook.

"There you are, girlie," said Jess, proffering the carrot which Polly knew had been lurking in Jess's pocket, "I expect Beckie will be out to see you shortly," she added, giving Polly a final hug before retracing her steps to the front door of Horwood House.

"Come in, dear," said Mrs Stockwood warmly. "Beckie's longing to meet you. I'll get you both something hot to drink – you must be cold after that ride on this chilly morning."

"Oh no, really – it's a lovely morning for riding."

"Well, I'll get you something anyway – and I'm sure you won't say no to one of my home-made cakes!" She led the way to a room at the front of the house. "Beckie's here, in the living room," she said. "You two get acquainted, while I fetch a tray." She opened the door. "Here we are, Beckie darling. Here's Jess."

It was a lovely room. The furnishings, of yellow and orange, seemed to echo the bright flames of the coal fire that burned brightly in the grate. Comfortable-looking chairs were drawn up to the fire and a small table stood to one side of where Beckie sat. Bright sunshine streamed in through the windows and the French door.

Mrs Stockwood left Jess, who stood awkwardly, just inside the door. It wasn't just that Jess felt suddenly shy at meeting this friend whom she had known only by correspondence. Jess was speechless as Beckie smiled up at her. For Beckie Stockwood was looking at her from a wheelchair.

Fourteen

"I should have told you," said Beckie, sipping at her coffee. She pushed the plate of cakes towards Jess. "Go on, have one. Mum will be disappointed if you don't. I think she's been looking forward to you coming over as much as I have! I was hoping to be out of this thing by now," Beckie explained, tapping the wheelchair with her hand, "but everything seems to take so long." She looked across the table at Jess. "I'm sorry I didn't say anything in my letters – did it surprise you to see me in a wheelchair?"

Jess suddenly felt very hungry. She chose a large slab of chocolate cake and bit into it. "Well . . . yes," she admitted. "I thought you must be feeling very weak with being in hospital for so long, and that was why you didn't come out to see Polly."

Beckie hesitated before she spoke. "I don't think I *will* come and see her – not . . . not this time. I want to wait until I can stand and walk properly – and *ride* her." She looked at Jess to see her reaction. "You must think I'm crazy! But I'd rather wait. I'll watch when you go—"

"But I thought – I thought – you wanted Polly . . ."

Beckie looked puzzled. Then, as she realised, her face was full of consternation. "Oh, Jess, I'm sorry. I didn't think. I didn't realise. You were bringing Polly back to me, weren't you – for good?"

Jess nodded. "Oh dear," Beckie sighed, "I don't seem to be getting anything right. I can't get walking yet. I want to *so* badly. And I want Polly back, too. But . . . but, I just want to get out of this thing. You understand, don't you?"

"Yes, I think I do," Jess replied slowly, remembering the feeling of cantering on Polly, the powerful body beneath her and the feeling that she was floating on air – flying almost. She could imagine how trapped Beckie felt, how she wanted to be free of the constraints of the chair before she even touched her beloved Polly again.

"I do, really I do," Jess repeated.

"So you don't mind taking Polly back and looking after her for a bit longer for me?"

Jess shook her head, laughing. "Of course not!"

Beckie's brown eyes were serious as she looked at Jess. "I think you feel the same about Polly as I do," she said, slowly, "and it must hurt to have to give her up after all these weeks. But I'll *share* her with you, Jess. And I'm sure you'll have your own pony one day – one just like Polly."

91

"Yes, one day . . ." Jess sighed and reached forward for another of Mrs Stockwood's delicious cakes.

So, there were still two ponies in the orchard at Trumpeter Cottage. Jess reminded herself, daily, that Polly would soon be gone for good.

"You see, Polly," Jess explained, from her usual seat on top of the orchard gate, "I'll be able to see you when I go to see Beckie. And, like Stan Croxford and Beckie said, I'll have my own pony one day – but it'll have to be just like you!"

"Can't I have a *little* ride on Muffin?" Tommy, sitting next to Jess, turned pleading eyes in her direction.

"Tom, you know what Mum said."

Tommy kicked at the gate. "But it's not fair," he wailed.

"Cheer up, Tommy," said Jess. "Mum and Dad will let you ride, I'm sure they will. One day, you'll ride and I'll have a pony that really is mine. We've just got to be patient." She jumped down from the gate. "Come on! Time to go – we're all off Christmas shopping this afternoon."

When Jess cycled over to Currington Bayley on the following morning, Beckie opened the front door from her wheelchair. Her eyes were shining.

"Doctor James is coming to see me on Monday," she told Jess excitedly. "I've been doing all my exercises – I'm sure he'll be pleased with me."

When Jess left, she arranged to visit Beckie later in the week, after the school term had finished.

It was just a week to Christmas. Life at Trumpeter Cottage was very busy. Christmas decorations were brought out from their boxes, and soon the cottage glittered and glowed with tinsel and paper chains. The Christmas tree, which had been chosen during the shopping trip, was carried into the lounge and decorated. Jess climbed one of the old apple trees in the orchard to retrieve some mistletoe from its topmost branches, and Dad cut armfuls of holly from the bush at the back of the orchard.

"Doesn't it look lovely!" Mum said on Sunday evening, when everyone had finished.

Jess looked round at it all – the decorations, the tree, Clare, Kim and Tommy propping up the Christmas cards, Badger flopped in front of the fire and the kittens chasing each other over the settee. She sighed with pleasure. Their first Christmas at Trumpeter Cottage was nearly here.

The school term finished on Wednesday morning. Jess changed from her school clothes into jeans and a sweater as soon as she arrived home.

"I'm going to see Beckie this afternoon," she informed her mother, "so can I get myself a quick lunch? Then I can be away from Beckie's home early and be home before dark. I'm taking her Christmas present."

"Yes, dear, of course – and why don't you ask Mrs Stockwood to bring Beckie over, now you're on holiday. I'm sure we could manage the wheelchair. The front door's quite wide, and those double doors into the lounge would easily give enough room."

"Great idea, Mum – I'll ask."

Jess hummed to herself as she cycled along the lanes to Currington Bayley. In the haversack on her back was Beckie's present – a large drawing block and a drawing pen.

At Horwood House, Jess propped her bicycle against the wall and rang the front door bell. Several minutes passed before the door was opened. It was Mrs Stockwood who stood in the doorway.

"Oh ... Jess ..." Mrs Stockwood's face looked drawn and tired. "I'm sorry, I didn't know you were coming. I'm afraid Beckie isn't well. I can't let you see her – I'm sorry, Jess."

Fifteen

Jess's return journey was much slower, as she puzzled over Beckie's sudden illness.

"What do you think is the matter, Mum?" she asked when she arrived home. "I didn't like to ask. Mrs Stockwood looked so worried."

"I'll ring her tomorrow," Mum promised. "Better not bother them today. Maybe it's a relapse. Beckie did have a very bad accident, you know."

Mum telephoned the next day and, after a long conversation with Mrs Stockwood, she returned to the kitchen looking thoughtful. "Don't worry," she told Jess, "Beckie's getting better . . . poor girl, she hasn't been very well. She's going to write to you as soon as she can."

"But Mum, she's all right, isn't she? What's the matter with her?"

"Let her tell you herself, Jessie," Mum replied, quietly.

The next few days leading up to Christmas were so full that Jess did not have much time to wonder about Beckie. There was more shopping, presents to wrap, mince pies to make and relatives to visit. Jess rode Polly and Muffin every day, and watched the post for a letter from Beckie, but nothing arrived.

Then, at last, it was Christmas Eve, with Tommy rushing excitedly around the lounge, Christmas carols, with Mum playing the piano, and everyone staying up later than usual.

Lying in bed at midnight, Jess listened to the church bells ringing. As she drifted off to sleep, she wondered how Beckie was feeling. But her last thought, as she fell asleep, was of Polly, quietly cropping the grass in the orchard, with Muffin.

"Wake up, Dess, wake up!"

It was Tommy, wide awake at half past five in the morning, tugging at Jess's sheet.

"Tommy, it's still night. I only just went to sleep."

"But it's Christmas, Dess. You haven't opened your stocking. Look what I had in mine!"

He blew screechingly down her ear through a toy trumpet – and Jess relinquished all hope of further sleep. She buried herself under her duvet and called out from her warm cave, "Tommy! I'll only get up if you stop that awful noise." The trumpet stopped.

"OK I give in," she said, emerging and sitting up in bed, yawning and groping for her Christmas stocking.

* * *

It was a family rule that no one opened the special presents around the Christmas tree until after breakfast.

"Come on – eat something sensible," Mum urged. "You can't all have a diet of chocolate Father Christmases!" But no one took much notice.

Dad had to be hauled from his Christmas lie-in, since it was another family rule that the whole family had to be there before presents were opened. Then began the handing over of presents, the frantic rustle and tear of paper and exclamations of delight.

Jess saved her present from Mum and Dad until last. There was a parcel and an envelope. Jess unwrapped the parcel.

"Oh, it's a lovely picture," she breathed, gazing at the beautiful, grey arab pony which looked out at her from the frame, its head thrown high and its mane lifting in the breeze. "It's just like Polly."

"That's what we thought," said Dad.

A squeal of delight came from the other side of the Christmas tree. Tommy was also opening his present from Mum and Dad. His round, pink, beaming face was topped by a small, black riding hat.

Jess looked towards her mother. "Does that mean—"

97

"Yes," Mum smiled. "I've given in. You can take Tommy out on Muffin. We're going to let him have some riding lessons, too."

Jess turned to her father. "But, Dad, is that all right . . . I mean . . . can you . . ."

"Yes, Jessie," Dad replied, anticipating her question. "Things are much better at work now. Mr Davies called me in last Monday. The firm has had a much better half-year – and I've been given that promotion at last!"

"Dad, that's wonderful!"

Jess turned her gaze to the picture of the grey arab. The more she looked at it, the more it looked like Polly, poised at the top of a hill, ready to canter down, her banner tail flowing behind her, her beautiful, fine head held proudly . . .

"Don't forget your other present," Mum said, pushing the envelope towards Jess.

Jess opened the envelope. Inside was a folded piece of paper. Opening it, Jess read:

> "If your present you want to find
> Out in the garden you must go.
> It's somewhere there if you just look
> So hurry up – don't be slow!"

"Whatever does this mean?" Jess asked, turning puzzled eyes towards her parents.

"Just what it says," said Dad, grinning at her. He caught hold of Tommy's hand. "Shall we go and help her, Tom?" he asked.

Kim and Clare gathered round, reading out the rhymed message. "What is it?" said Kim. "Some flowers, do you think?"

"A tree!" suggested Tommy.

"Or a lake!" stated the more ambitious Clare.

"Don't you know either?" asked Jess. The two girls shook their heads.

"Come on!" shrieked an excited Tommy, "a treasure hunt!"

The whole family, including Badger and the kittens, followed Jess into the garden. Badger thought that they were all quite crazy, and stood with puzzled eyes and gently waving tail, watching the four Caswell children wander up and down the garden, peering at the ground and up at the trees. The three kittens thought that this was a glorious new game and spent their time leaping out at the children and each other from behind the cabbages.

"I can't see anything," Jess admitted.

"Nor me," agreed Kim.

"I'm cold," said Clare.

A shrill whinny sounded from the direction of the orchard.

"It's Polly," said Jess. "She's heard us." She hurried in the direction of the orchard, but when she rounded the corner by the coal shed, she came to an abrupt standstill.

"What's Polly doing in the stable?" Jess exclaimed.

"And what's that flapping on her neck?" said Kim. Jess hurried over to the stable. Polly whinnied again – a soft, welcoming sound – as Jess approached. She pawed the ground impatiently.

Jess put her arm round the pony's neck. "You don't like being in here, do you, girlie? You're used to the orchard." Her hand touched something – a piece of card. "Whatever . . ." Around Polly's neck was a piece of string and attached to the string was a large Christmas card. Looking inside, Jess read, "Happy Christmas, to Jess with love from Mum and Dad."

Jess felt herself go pale. It couldn't mean what it seemed to mean. It wasn't possible. She must be misunderstanding. She swung round. There were Mum and Dad, smiling at her.

"Happy Christmas, Jess," said Dad.

"But . . . but . . ."

"She's yours, Jessie," said Mum. "Polly's yours."

"But . . . she can't be. Polly belongs to Beckie . . ." Jess felt close to tears. She had just been told that she could have what she wanted more than anything else in the world, but it didn't seem possible. She wondered, briefly, whether she was having a tortured dream and soon she would wake. Polly nudged her shoulder. She felt real enough.

Mum stepped closer. "She really *is* yours now, Jess," she repeated, gently. "It was Beckie's idea.

She was determined about it, once she decided. She had some bad news, you see, last Monday – from Doctor James. That's why she wouldn't see you on Wednesday."

"But, what—"

"Doctor James told Beckie that she may never walk again. They kept hoping and hoping at the hospital, but . . . well, now they think that her back is too damaged."

"But, Mum, that's awful. I can't take Polly away from her – especially now."

Mrs Caswell put an arm around her daughter's shoulders. "Beckie was desperately upset when she was told," she explained. "She's coming over after lunch – and Mr and Mrs Stockwood. They're staying to tea. She didn't write a letter after all, because she wanted you to have a surprise."

As they walked slowly back to the cottage, Jess continued to question her mother. "How long have you known about this, Mum?" she asked.

"Only since Thursday, when I spoke to Mrs Stockwood on the phone. Beckie was absolutely determined about it, she said. They wouldn't take the proper amount for Polly, either. Beckie said that it *must* be you who had Polly – otherwise she couldn't bear to part with her."

For the rest of the morning, Jess divided her time between helping Mum with the vegetables, and gazing disbelievingly at Polly, who was back in the orchard with Muffin. Christmas lunch was a ritual which she hardly noticed. She *had* to see Beckie.

At four o'clock, the Stockwoods' car drove down the drive and came to a halt outside the front door. The two sets of parents greeted each other and Mr Stockwood took the wheelchair from the boot of the car. Then he lifted Beckie out and sat her in the chair. Beckie waved to Jess, who hung back.

"Happy Christmas, Jess!" She waved a parcel in Jess's direction. As Jess came up, she said, before Jess had a chance to speak, "Take me to see Polly, *please*, Jess." Then, thrusting the parcel into her hands, she added, "and I hope you like this."

"Thanks." Jess was glad to be able to grasp the wheelchair handle and escape the watching eyes of the parents. "You shouldn't have," she added.

"Of course I should, silly!" said Beckie, laughing. "Your present was super – just what I wanted. I'm going to draw a lot more from now on – that's one of the things I decided this week. I really love drawing, and I think I want to be an artist."

"Your drawings are really good," Jess told her, as she guided the chair carefully over the path leading to the stable. Beckie could use the chair herself, but the uneven ground made it hard work. Jess sat on the wall while she opened the parcel from Beckie.

"Beckie! How did you know?" Jess examined the grooming kit delightedly. "I've only got an old dandy brush that Rachel let me have when I looked after Beetle." She pulled out the contents. "Look! Even a comb – I'll be able to comb Polly's tail . . . Beckie!"

"Yes?"

"I can't take Polly from you."

"Why not?" demanded Beckie. "It seems sensible to me."

"Sensible?"

"Yes. Don't you see?" Beckie paused. Then she began again, talking quickly. "Now look. I love Polly. I want to ride her. But I can't. I just *can't*. It's no good beating about the bush. If I don't walk again, I shan't be able to ride her again – ever."

"But people do ride ponies," Jess put in, "disabled people, I mean."

"I know," Beckie replied. "I asked Doctor James about it. But he said that it would be a long time before I could – and even then I would have to go to a special centre, where they have helpers and very quiet ponies."

Beckie, who had been looking down as she spoke, looked up now. Despite the seriousness of her eyes, she smiled ruefully. "Neither of us can say that Polly is quiet and docile, can we? Much as we love her and know how gorgeous she is to ride, we both know that she's . . . well, flighty, at times!" Grudgingly, Jess agreed.

"You know when you came on Wednesday," Beckie continued. Jess nodded. "Well, I had been crying for two days – since Doctor James came and told me. Then, when Mum told me that you'd been – well, I stopped at last! And then I started thinking. And then Doctor James came again." Beckie chuckled. "He said he had given me the normal two days for crying! He's really nice," she added, seriously. "We had a long talk, and that's when I realised that *you* must have Polly."

"But I still don't—"

"Jess, I *know* how you feel about Polly because I feel the same. I saw you, you see, when you brought Polly to me when I came back from hospital. I saw you have a good howl when you thought you were saying goodbye to Polly. Well, that's just what I did, too. And I really am saying goodbye to *riding* Polly. But I'm lucky because I shall be able to see her any time by coming to see you."

"Or I'll bring her to see you."

"That's right." Beckie paused. "And I was hoping that you and Polly would help me to live with this," she added, looking down at the wheelchair.

105

Jess was quiet for a moment. Then she said, slowly, "I'll go and fetch her, then, shall I?"

Beckie grinned. "Great!"

Collecting the head-collar from the shed, Jess made her way to the orchard, where Polly and Muffin waited, expectantly. They had heard the voices.

"I'll be there shortly with a feed," Jess promised Muffin as she slipped the head-collar on to Polly.

Jess opened the gate and the grey pony stepped daintily through the muddy opening, looking about her eagerly and snorting in the crisp December air.

"Polly!" Beckie called, and the grey arab whickered. "Oh, Jess, she's even lovelier when you haven't seen her for six months."

Polly pranced sideways, snorting noisily and eyeing the wheelchair with suspicion.

"You'll have to get used to it, Polly," Beckie told her. "It's going to be with us for a long time."

"Beckie."

Beckie turned to her friend. "Yes?"

"Let's share her. Let Polly be ours."

Beckie laughed. "Jess Caswell, when will I make you understand? OK," she added. "We'll say that Polly is ours. But I've had my turn – now it's yours."

Beckie smiled up at Jess, but her eyes were serious as she spoke again.

"She's yours now, Jess."

Wendy Douthwaite
All Because of Polly £2.99

Having her own pony is a dream come true for Jess, and everything
she ever wanted. Life seems perfect – until Polly gets ill and nearly
dies. As Jess and her family fight for Polly's life, they have no idea just
what her recovery will mean. For Jess it is a true happy ending, and for
her friend Beckie, confined to a wheelchair after a car crash, it is the
most important thing that could *ever* have happened.